Happy reading
Alton Towers.

CJElliott

W.V.J ELLIOTT

Matador
9 Priory Business Park,
Wistow Road, Kibworth Beauchamp,
Leicestershire. LE8 0RX
Tel: 0116 279 2299
Email: books@troubador.co.uk
Web: www.troubador.co.uk/matador
Twitter: @matadorbooks

ISBN 978 1785890 659

British Library Cataloguing in Publication Data.
A catalogue record for this book is available from the British Library.

Printed and bound in the UK by TJ International, Padstow, Cornwall
Typeset in 14pt Bookman Old Style by Troubador Publishing Ltd, Leicester, UK

Matador is an imprint of Troubador Publishing Ltd

This book is dedicated to:

My wonderful husband Gary, for his endless love, support and patience.

&

To my daddy, who I miss dearly and who inspired me with his love of magic and encouraged my creative mind.

Acknowledgements:

Thank you to my children Niki, Lee and Paul, of whom I am so proud, for giving me the excuse to make up nonsense bedtime stories when they were little.

To Cassy, Luke and Lauren, for their love and support.

Debbie Bellaby, my illustrator, who brought my characters to life – perfectly.

To my best friend Dawn, for believing in me.

And finally to my imagination because without that, writing my stories wouldn't have been half as much fun.

Introduction

Welcome to the story of Ellimas, a day that celebrates the birth of springtime and the promise of summer. Ellimas is kept very much a secret and a celebration, which only fairy folk enjoy. But if you listen very carefully I will unfold the secrets of Ellimas, open the doors to Mallowbrook Hollow and introduce you to a special kind of fairy folk called dewbies.

Fairies are beautiful and childlike. They are also very fast and use their tiny little wings to carry themselves up and over the flowers in our gardens. Fairies never lie and it is said that their magic enables them to grant the deepest of human wishes.

Fairies collect our wishes and take them to the Enchanted Wishing Well and only when the wishing well believes your wish to be genuine and true, is a fairy able to grant it.

If you are ever fortunate enough to meet a fairy, be sure to say hello politely and treat them kindly because fairies are very shy and before granting your wishes they need to trust that you will bring them no harm.

The wisest, most deserving of all fairies become tooth fairies, who are responsible for exchanging children's unwanted teeth for coins.

Pixies are mischievous and naughty. They are known to gather in large groups at the bottom of our gardens at night for dancing and singing. Pixies are at their happiest when they are having fun, which they prefer to do instead of working.

They have pale green skin that sparkles when they are happy, long pointed noses and large ears.

Good pixies are kind to humans, helping with unfinished work or the household chores whilst we sleep.

Elves are little fairy folk with pointed ears and magical powers. They can be quite unpredictable and their moods change quickly.

They are not afraid of humans and are happy to watch us from their secret hideaways, tucked in the corners of our homes and gardens.

Elves, like pixies, are helpful to humans but sometimes, because they are so eager to assist, they get too excited and their good intentions go wrong.

Gnomes are small creatures who mainly live underground, guarding the Earth's buried treasure. It is said that they are very hard working and great inventors.

At night time, whilst we sleep, gnomes are busy working in our gardens caring for the plants and flowers. They are also best friends to all of the garden animals and insects.

Gnomes do not have magical powers but it is said that they can protect humans from evil magic.

eprechauns are thrifty and extremely clever. They spend their time making and mending shoes. It is said that they are very wealthy and hide all of their coins in a hidden pot of gold at the end of the rainbow. If you spot a leprechaun you must never take your eyes off of him, for he can vanish in an instant. But should you catch a leprechaun, he has the magical power to grant you three wishes in exchange for his freedom. A leprechaun may steal or borrow almost anything, so if you find yourself looking for a missing object and can't find it anywhere, it might be that you have not misplaced it but that a leprechaun has taken it away with him.

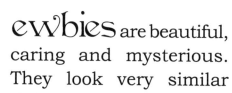ewbies are beautiful, caring and mysterious. They look very similar to fairies but do not have wings and love nothing more than to feel the sunshine on their little faces. Each dewbie owns their own dragonfly, which helps them to fly around our gardens. They sprinkle fresh dewdrops onto plants and flower petals first thing in the morning, just as the sun peeps through the night sky. Each dewdrop is filled with a dewbie's sweetest thoughts. When they are happy the tiny droplets are as clear as the purest water and sparkle like the most precious of diamonds. If a dewbie becomes sad or lonely, their dewdrops become cloudy and grey, which is said to reflect their unhappy feelings. Dewbies are very busy between springtime and summer and this is the time when they are most

at risk of being spotted by humans. During autumn and winter, Jack Frost takes over their work by covering the flowers and plants with a cold dusting of sparkling ice crystals. Unlike fairies, who move from human to human granting wishes and collecting teeth, when a dewbie is considered old and wise enough they can leave Mallowbrook Hollow. Should they then choose to live at the bottom of your garden they will stay with you forever.

 **D**ragonflies are used for their elegance and speed. If you are lucky enough to see one in your garden look very, very closely; you may just see a dewbie sitting across its back, riding it like a pony and dashing around the flowers and plants sprinkling them with morning dew as they fly past. Dragonflies shimmer with many different colours. When a dewbie is introduced to their dragonfly for the very first time, a special magic happens between them; whatever colour the dragonfly chooses to be on that particular day, as soon as the dewbie sits across its back, in a flash their clothes become the same colour as their new pet. This is the colour that unites them for the rest of their lives together.

It is believed that if you look deep into a dragonfly's tear, you will

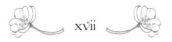

see your future unfold before you. Dragonflies do not cry freely and it is considered a rare honour if this ever happens to a human.

Caterfiddles are beetle like insects. They have a hard shell and strong wings but have the face of a caterpillar, with big brown eyes, soft fur and long antenna, which look like curly eyelashes. They are used for their speed and strength and only the most important of fairy folk use these unusual creatures to travel around our gardens. Caterfiddles are invisible to humans but as they fly their wings create a mist of sweet perfume. So, whilst in your garden, if your nose is ever filled with an unexplained scent only then will you know that one is close by.

 eenarks were fairies many years ago. They used their magic selfishly to gain beauty, wealth and power-never using their magic for the good of humans. So Arlik, the king of the elves, removed their magic. He replaced their bright and colourful clothes with shabby dark cloth; clipped their wings so they could not fly; and banished them to the darkest, coldest corner of the Weeping Woods as punishment for their selfish ways. Neenarks believe that their curse will be lifted if they drink a dewdrop from a fresh young oak leaf. However, dewbies do not venture into the Weeping Woods. So the oak leaves remain old and dry and the neenarks remain forgotten forever.

Chapter 1

In an enchanted garden called Mallowbrook Hollow, fairies, pixies, elves, gnomes, leprechauns, dewbies and all kinds of fairy folk can be found, living happily together. By day the fairy folk children, under the watchful eye of Arlik, learn the importance of keeping their existence a secret. They also learn how their special kind of magic helps both humans and Mother Nature; but most importantly of all they learn how to be helpful, kind and honest.

Between the hours of dusk and dawn the fairy folk sneak into the gardens and houses of humans, spreading their magic and being very careful not to be seen or, even worse, caught.

Elliot is a dewbie. She lives in Mallowbrook Hollow with her parents Dawn and Ludo, her sister Echo and her brother Bear. Elliot has a round little face, with rosy pink cheeks, long auburn hair, a tiny nose and big brown eyes. Elliot loves the colour yellow because it reminds her of the summer and because she shares this colour with Nelson, her dragonfly. Her mother always makes sure she has a big yellow bow tied at her waist and yellow ribbons in her hair.

Dawn, Elliot's mother, is kind and beautiful and was given her name because dawn is the time of day when dewbies are at their busiest, covering the land in fresh dew. She has long blonde hair, which she ties in braids and wraps around the top of her head, like a crown of shimmering gold.

The colour she shares with Skyler, her dragonfly, is blue-chosen for peace and wisdom. Dawn has patience and is wise to the stubbornness of her husband Ludo. She often catches him smiling under his large bushy grey beard, whilst he is trying his hardest to be serious with her and their children.

Ludo is head dewbie and he looks after the safety of Arlik and his queen Lillianna. Ludo is strong and serious and is always on guard. He wears the colour red, chosen for strength, and rides a caterfiddle called Storm.

Elliot loves her father. He makes her giggle when he twitches his

3

pointed nose and when his round cheeks blush a bright scarlet when he is cross. To Elliot he is a soldier, a warrior and her hero. But she also knows him to be soft and gentle, especially when he appears to be fast asleep, with his eyes closed tight underneath his big bushy eyebrows. Elliot likes to sneak up close to watch him sleeping but somehow he always seems to know she is there. When she moves in close to kiss him gently on the top of his head, he opens one of his big blue eyes, which always makes her jump, and they fall about laughing.

Elliot's younger brother and sister are twins but not identical. Echo looks similar to Elliot, with auburn hair and a round little face, however Echo's eyes are the brightest blue just like their father's. She has his stubbornness too. Dawn often tells Echo that she will make a great leader one day, just like her father. Bear is

shorter than Echo with thick curly black hair, big brown eyes and a little turned up nose covered in freckles. He gives Elliot the best cuddles of all.

Both Echo and Bear are not quite old enough to have their own dragonflies but as a treat Ludo often takes them with him when he rides Storm. The twins scream with delight as they all fly around Mallowbrook Hollow at great speed.

Dixie and Boo are Elliot's best friends and the girls spend all of their spare time together.

Dixie is slightly shorter and plumper than her friends, with red curly hair and the biggest, brightest green eyes you have ever seen. Dixie's hair reminds Elliot of tight springs, all waiting to break free from the large orange bow she ties around them. Dixie's favourite colour is orange, which is a good choice because it matches both her bright hair and Bouncer, her dragonfly.

Boo is pretty in every way and she reminds Elliot of a princess. She has twinkling blue eyes and long straight hair, which looks almost silver in the sunshine. Boo tucks her hair neatly behind her pointed ears and always leaves it untied and free to flow loosely down her back. She has a tiny button nose, rose pink lips and a graceful elegance about her. Boo's dragonfly is called Fluster, who is the softest shade of pale green making him almost invisible as they weave through the plants and flowers.

Chapter 2

Elliot is a daydreamer and is often found sleeping under a large toadstool, which is situated deep in the heart of Mallowbrook. On this particular day, early one December morning, Elliot had escaped the Christmas preparations and was lying in the semi-shade, her head propped up on the stem of the toadstool, dreaming about the seasons and what she liked most about them.

Spring

Elliot's first thoughts drifted to springtime, a time when Mallowbrook Hollow was filled with excitement; the long dark nights had disappeared, the last of the frost had settled, animals

were venturing out of their winter homes and the plants and trees were dressed in fresh, green shoots. Everything had a newness about it and everyone was happy.

The first dawn of springtime signals the first morning dew. Each dewbie eagerly climbs aboard their dragonfly ready to coat the grasses, fields, plants and trees with a sprinkling of the sweetest dewdrops, from their tiny silver spoons. Elliot loved nothing more than to climb onto Nelson and fly with the cool spring breeze, just like a surfer riding the highest of waves, up and over the newly awakened plants.

Each spring, dewbies far and wide arrive at Mallowbrook Hollow for the annual Dragonfly Giving Day. Elliot was especially looking forward to the next one because Echo and Bear, her brother and sister, would be old enough to receive their own dragonflies.

At a certain age, and once dewbie training is well underway, youngsters are given the responsibility of their very own dragonfly. Each of the children who are being presented wears a headdress of woven grasses and a long cloak, made out of the finest silk.

The ceremony starts with the children parading around the Old Maple Tree in the middle of Mallowbrook Meadow, to merry tunes played by the pixies. Then, the audience of dewbies waits in silent anticipation for the magic to happen as each child is lifted very carefully upon the back of their dragonfly. After a few seconds pass, from a cloud of shimmering dragonfly dust, the child and its pet emerges in the brightest of colour. The colour is chosen by the dragonfly and this is the colour which will unite them forever. The crowd clap and cheer as they watch the youngsters nervously ride their

dragonflies for the first time and the somewhat awkward landings when the first flights are over.

The arrival of spring seals the promise of summer and this, for Elliot, was the best feeling of all.

Summer

Elliot sighed deeply at remembering the feeling of the warm sunshine on her face and the outside fun shared with her friends. Classes with Arlik only last until mid-morning, so each day when school finishes the friends take a picnic of fresh berries to their secret summer hideaway and lay on the warm grass talking, laughing, playing and dozing in the shade. Their camp is underneath an old metal dustbin lid, which over the years had positioned itself between two tree stumps, allowing the friends to crawl underneath it and out of sight. Elliot especially enjoys listening to the

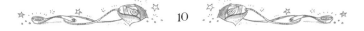

summer rain drops bounce over the metal lid. The friends giggle as they make up nonsense songs to sing in time with the delicate ting, ting tune.

The girls spend warm summer days making long winding daisy chains, which they drape carefully around their camp, and picking the brightest of buttercup flowers, which they turn upside down to make sun hats.

Pebble hopping across the small stream that runs through the Hollow is another summer pastime that the friends enjoy and one which takes great skill and concentration. One at a time they collect a handful of tiny pebbles; then, from the grassy bank on the river's edge they each throw the first of their tiny stones and hop onto it, being very careful not to slip on its wet shiny surface. The winner is the first friend to use all of their pebbles to reach the other side without falling into the stream,

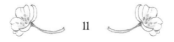

which unfortunately Elliot has never managed to do. Unlike Dixie and Boo, who hop onto their pebbles with the lightest and most graceful of steps, Elliot runs at the pebbles with speed, landing on each one with a clumsy bump followed by a tumble into the cool water. The sight of Elliot sitting in the stream, wet and covered in riverweeds, always makes Dixie and Boo fall about with laughter.

Summer seemed to fill everyone with happiness in Mallowbrook and Elliot often wondered whether she would enjoy this time of year as much when she was old enough to leave and set up a new home in her own human's garden.

Autumn

Autumn is Elliot's least favourite season of all. The onset of autumn seemed to draw a line under the summer for another year and this made Elliot sad. Mallowbrook Hollow is at its busiest, with fairy folk preparing for the winter months ahead-this activity known to them as Nootling. Berries and seeds are gathered; makeshift homes are being patched with moss and leaves to keep them free from the icy winds; and glow worms are plucked from the ground ready for the cold winter nights. The leprechauns are busy

making waterproof shoes; gnomes are working hard in our gardens preparing the plants and garden animals for the determined winter weather ahead; and the pixies dance, just as they always do.

Elliot and her family live inside an old disused metal watering can, which has positioned itself upside down on top of a retired compost heap. The front door, which a gnome friend of Ludo's made from an old bottle top, is fixed to the top of the spout. Once through the bottle top door, entry into the home is made by climbing up the spout and exit is made by sliding all the way down; needless to say the children prefer to exit! The soft compost provides a warm cosy carpet and the tiny rust holes, which have appeared over time, let enough daylight through to brighten up the inside.

It was the winter storms, which caused the most damage-rusting away patches of the old metal and leaving

behind large ugly holes. One of Elliot's jobs in the autumn is to help her father to collect soft moss and leaves, so that Ludo can fill the holes making their little home 'winter proof' again. Elliot has a little corner of the watering can all to herself and when the winter nights creep in, she often lies on her bed of warm, soft bird feathers and peeks out through one of the little rust holes at the darkness outside, feeling extremely lucky to be tucked up inside their cosy little home.

At the time between autumn's close and winter's opening, fairy folk hold their Nootlenarlie celebrations: the autumn carnival. This festival celebrates the passing of the spring and summer months and an end to all of the Nootling, which has been done in the autumn. It is a time for relaxation, dancing and singing. All around the world in our gardens, one night each year, fairy folk spread the fallen leaves into a large circle and inside of this circle the celebrations are held. Before sitting down to a feast of wild berries and nuts, the fairy folk children take part in the Light Procession. Each child holds a tiny firefly cupped in their hands to light the way and skips around the circle of leaves, whilst elves play merry tunes on their flutes made out of dried reed. This procession is then followed by the Dance Of The Dewbies and as they weave and move in time to the music, they shower the circle in sparkling

dew drops, which is said to look just like millions of crystals falling from the sky. Once the children have gone off to bed, the adults dance and sing until dawn, filling their bellies with the tasty food and drinking warm honey from acorn shells.

So, if a mysterious circle of scattered leaves ever appears at the bottom of your garden, you'll know that Nootlenarlie has been celebrated.

Winter

Elliot loves the wintertime because there is less work to do and more time for fun and games with her best friends Dixie and Boo. Elliot especially enjoyed: the heat from the glow worms, as her family snuggle around them to keep warm on a cold winter's night; skating on the frozen puddles; snowball fights; and, of course, Christmas. Elliot loved Christmas the best of all. Hanging

the decorations around Mallowbrook Hollow, exchanging presents and the big Christmas party held by Arlik and his queen Lillianna, underneath the Forgotten Sundial.

Elliot liked Lillianna. She was beautiful and kind, with floor length blonde hair, which glistened like strands of gold. She had a crown made out of twisted willow bark and a long flowing gown in the deepest of purples. As she walked, fairy dust fell from her footsteps and sunbeams lit up her path. Everyone loved Lillianna and smiled with pride, as they swept her a bow when blessed with her company. Lillianna's wings were the biggest and most colourful fairy wings Elliot had ever seen and she often wondered why she never used them to fly. Lillianna always carried her wings tightly to her back, all neat and tidy. Only on very rare occasions did Elliot see them shudder ever so slightly, as if to get themselves

comfortable once again and this always made Elliot giggle.

At Christmas time Arlik and Lillianna give everyone in Mallowbrook a gift. The presents are placed carefully on top of a large toadstool, which sits proudly in the shade underneath the Forgotten Sundial. Present giving at Mallowbrook is the most amazing and wonderful sight to see. As the fairy folk gather under the Forgotten Sundial, each of the guests are given a snowdrop full of the sweetest nectar whilst they wait for the arrival of Arlik and Lillianna. When the procession begins the birds sing, frogs croak, beetles click, the wings of the hummingbirds hum and everyone claps and dances in time to the music, especially the pixies who love to dance. The Christmas decorations glisten in the winter sunshine, dewdrops are hung on strands like twinkling fairy lights and the mouth-watering feast of mistletoe and holly berries is carefully laid out on the mushroom tables, ready to be eaten.

The food looks temptingly tasty and the procession takes so long, that Echo and Bear often have to be reminded by their father not to touch the food until they are told to do so, which always makes Echo sulk.

On one particular Christmas Eve a few years ago, Elliot and her friends, Dixie and Boo, decided to venture to the Forgotten Sundial to take a secret peek at the presents and decorations before everyone else arrived the next day. The friends knew that the Forgotten Sundial was a forbidden place to go on Christmas Eve but their excitement took over and in an instant they had jumped aboard their dragonflies, Nelson, Bouncer and Fluster, and flew towards the sundial.

As the friends arrived, they could

see the pile of carefully placed presents balancing on top of the large toadstool, each one wrapped in shiny sweet wrappers, collected from our gardens by gnomes throughout the year. All was quiet, yet magical and full of anticipation waiting for the Christmas parade and party, which would be held the very next day. The girls flew high and low, chasing each other up and around, trying to dislodge the perfectly wrapped presents, hoping that one would break open so they could peek inside. They giggled with enjoyment whilst darting through the strings of decorations, knocking the dewdrops gently together to make a clinking sound.

It was only when their game had come to an end and they had landed their dragonflies onto the soft moss of the ground, that they saw Arlik.

Arlik had been watching them with amusement, his arms folded over

his round belly and a smile secretly hidden behind his long beard and now he stood before them waiting for an explanation. The girls blushed the brightest red and dropped their heads knowing just how much trouble they were in. Elliot squeezed her eyes shut tight and the friends stood side by side holding hands in preparation for Arlik's lecture but without a word, he peered at them from under his bushy grey eyebrows, gave them a twinkling wink and walked away. It was Christmas Eve after all, a time for forgiveness and this occasion was no exception.

Arlik, just like Elliot, adored the magic of Christmas time and having no children of his own he held a special place in his heart for Elliot. He admired her enjoyment of life, loved her spirit of adventure, adored her sweet and honest nature but most of all, she shared his love of Christmas and he looked after her just like he

would have done for one of his own children.

Elliot's birthday fell in late January, the deepest of winter, when the nights are long and the days are short and when Mallowbrook Hollow is left dormant and untouched. The animals have long gone into hibernation, wrapped up inside their nests and burrows all cosy and warm and Jack Frost is busy each morning, coating the countryside in ice crystals.

Elliot enjoys her birthday but with every wish she has made whilst blowing out the candles on previous birthday cakes, she'd wished that just once she could celebrate her special day in the spring or summer. Elliot longed for a birthday in the meadow, with her friends, feeling the warm grass tickle beneath their bare feet and being able to dance and play in the sunshine. Dawn and Ludo see the sadness in Elliot's eyes each birthday, when she is forced to

remain inside by the warmth of the glow worms, watching the soft snow flakes fall from heavy grey skies outside, envious of the other children who celebrate their birthdays in the summer. Knowing this, each year they try their very best to fill her day with gifts and enjoyment and always plan a special 'inside' birthday party with her best friends.

Chapter 3

Elliot was quickly woken from her semi slumber by a brisk winter's breeze, which had circled around her face. She gave a large yawn and with tired eyes peered out from underneath the toadstool. Although only mid-afternoon, the sky was dark and heavy, which signalled time for Elliot to head for home. As she ventured outside, the angry clouds began to release their store of rain and large droplets fell from the sky. Elliot grabbed a fallen acorn leaf and held it above her head as a makeshift umbrella and skipped around the dusty puddles, which were now forming on the ground.

On her journey, she bumped into Dixie and Boo who had also been

caught in the rain. The friends all huddled underneath Elliot's umbrella leaf and headed off to their secret hideaway, which was closest.

By the time they had reached the old dustbin lid, the rain was at its heaviest. The familiar ting, ting sound of summer raindrops had been replaced with a loud clattering, which sounded like a hundred acorns bouncing across the top of their camp.

The breeze was stronger now and a cold, icy mist was blowing around Mallowbrook making the Hollow appear eerie and uninviting. Their den felt unfamiliar and unwelcoming, void of the usual surroundings of warmth and daisy chains.

Several hours passed and it was late afternoon when the rain slowed to a steady sprinkle and the friends were able to break their boredom and venture outside again. The air was fresh, the sky was brighter and the Hollow appeared clean and sparkling, as if a spring clean had just taken place. The girls stood for a moment, enjoying the coolness of the drizzle as it dusted their faces and the damp grass as it chilled their bare feet. It was only when a nightingale's sweet song echoed from high in the tree top above that their trance was disturbed and they noticed the most unusual sight in the far distance.

A   rainbow   had   presented

itself before them, arching in a multi-coloured spectacular across Mallowbrook Hollow and the friends knew exactly what this meant; for when a rainbow appears, it is said that a leprechaun has hidden their gold coins in a pot at the very end. Leprechauns summon the appearance of a rainbow when they have saved so much gold that they can hardly carry it all.

The friends all knew that rainbows were very rare and because their recent boredom had sparked a sense of adventure within them, they decided that they would investigate this further.

The girls each pulled from their pocket a whistler and held it up to their mouths blowing into them as hard as they could. Whistlers are old snail shells, which are used by dewbies to summon their dragonflies. Elliot blew into her whistler, which made a sweet hooting sound and in

an instant Nelson arrived at her side. As Dixie blew into her whistler it gave a loud pip, pip calling Bouncer, who appeared suddenly in a bright orange mist. Finally, with an almighty honk, honk of Boo's whistler, Fluster arrived and landed in an untidy heap of legs and wings at her feet. Fluster was the clumsiest of all dragonflies.

One by one, the friends climbed aboard their pets and sped off into the heart of the Hollow towards their prize: the brightest, most colourful rainbow they had ever seen.

Chapter 4

It continued to rain lightly, creating a swirling mist forcing the girls to race each other high over the tree tops, looking downwards at the white cloud which had now covered Mallowbrook in a fluffy blanket. Their pace became faster and faster and their adventure became a race as each one desperately tried to reach the rainbow first. Rainbows, however, are cunning and followers are fooled by the illusion that they appear just in reach. No matter how far you travel and how close you think you are, they never get any closer and Elliot was left wondering if leprechauns were the only ones to know their secret.

Determined, and now somewhat frustrated, Elliot beckoned Nelson to

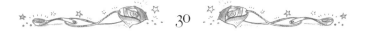

fly faster and faster. She became so far in front that Dixie and Boo could not see her through the mist, which had now circled its way upwards. Elliot was unaware that in their quest to catch up, Fluster, who was unable to see clearly and who was leading the way, had actually led her friends in the opposite direction and they were in fact heading homewards instead.

Elliot and Nelson continued to gallop with speed. Preoccupied with their mission, it was only when the rain had stopped and the rainbow was fading fast that Elliot noticed the cold darkness, which was following her and Nelson as they flew. Looking around her, she realised that her friends were not behind and that the thick mist had now hidden the bright colours of the rainbow. The familiar surroundings of Mallowbrook Hollow were gone and everywhere became quiet and eerie. Elliot felt lost and lonely, especially as a cold panic

churned inside her belly, realising that she was unable to slow Nelson, who was still charging through the dark icy fog.

Elliot could feel Nelson's heaving panting as she threw her arms tightly around his neck, trying really hard to stay upright on his back. As the pair flew out of the mist and into a land, which was both unfamiliar and uninviting, Nelson did not see the old oak tree they were heading straight for. Unable to pull Nelson to a sharp

halt, they hit the old tree with an uncontrolled crash and tumbled through a large hole, which had been carved into the decaying wood by a woodpecker many years before. Down and down they fell, twisting and turning in the darkness, landing with a sharp bump as they hit the damp, dusty floor of the tree's trunk.

When Elliot opened her eyes several minutes later, she was blinded by the darkness; her eyes were unable to focus and on touch, nothing around her felt familiar, except Nelson, who was breathing slowing beside her in a dazed slumber.

Elliot glanced upwards and through squinted eyes, could just make out the starry night sky, skimming the hole she guessed they had just fallen through. A wave of tiredness overwhelmed Elliot and she allowed her eyes to close once again, shutting out the blackness around her. With a deep sigh, unable to fight

the wooziness which had filled her head, Elliot snuggled underneath one of Nelson's large wings, close to the warmth of his soft skin and drifted into a deep sleep.

Chapter 5

The winter night sky had crept in by the time Dixie and Boo had arrived outside Elliot's home. Ludo was outside pacing up and down in an angry stomp, with worry etched across his bright red face and as he looked up and saw the two girls minus his daughter, he demanded an explanation.

In a flurry of mixed words and sadness, the girls told Ludo of their adventure and how, because of the mist, they had lost track of Elliot who had disappeared into the fog and out of sight. They went on to explain that Boo's brave and clever dragonfly, Fluster, managed to bring them back home to safety, even though at times the fog was dense and their journey scary. Ludo's pacing stopped and it

was replaced by a stillness, leaving the girls to wonder whether he was so cross he was unable to speak or frozen to the spot with sheer worry. The crinkles which appeared on his forehead and the tiny tear which had escaped from one of his eyes told the girls that he was worried, very worried indeed, and the girls started to cry.

The crying soon stirred the other members of Elliot's household and Dawn, followed closely by Echo and Bear, swiftly appeared from the spout of their watering can house. Ludo ushered the twins back inside the safety of their home whilst quickly explaining to Dawn the story of their daughter's disappearance. He then pulled a whistler from the chest pocket of his red tunic and blew breathlessly into it summoning Storm, his Caterfiddle. On the sound of Ludo's whistle, Storm landed with a hard thump at Ludo's side and in no time at all, they were heading

off towards Arlik's palace to gather assistance from the other soldier dewbies and elves. Dawn was left standing in front of their tiny home, in a breeze of caterfiddle mist, with her arms folded tightly around Elliot's friends. She knew that if anyone could find their precious daughter, her husband Ludo, the strongest, bravest dewbie in all of the land, would be able to.

News of Elliot's disappearance spread quickly through the kingdom and Arlik's soldiers were eager to help with the search, including Arlik himself, much to the disapproval of Ludo, who wanted him to stay in the safety of the palace. As the soldiers climbed aboard their caterfiddles, Arlik declared that every corner, every nook, the length and breadth of Mallowbrook Hollow was to be searched and as Arlik's words drifted off into the darkness of the night, Ludo signalled for the search to begin.

The search for Elliot carried on throughout the night and every corner of the Hollow was investigated without success. As the winter sun rose on this crisp mid-December morning, an army of weary soldiers returned to the castle tired and hungry. Ludo was exhausted with concern and desperately wanted to carry on looking for his daughter but Arlik ordered him home to rest and after an unsuccessful protest, Ludo returned to his family and fell fast asleep in his favourite chair.

As the days went by and no news of Elliot had arrived, the fairy folk of Mallowbrook Hollow fell into a sad daze. Every waking moment was spent by Ludo and willing volunteers looking for fresh clues as to Elliot's whereabouts and Dawn was trying her hardest to keep herself both busy and happy for the sake of Echo and Bear, who were forever asking where their big sister was.

Christmas was fast approaching

and it became very obvious to Arlik and Lillianna that the annual hustle and bustle underneath the Forgotten Sundial was missing. The sundial appeared dull and unloved, bare of festive decorations and lacked the usual joy and merriment of folk preparing for the Christmas party. This year was very different and Arlik felt a pang of sadness as he remembered how much Elliot enjoyed Christmas and how it wouldn't be the same without her being with them.

An announcement quickly followed from the palace; Christmas at Mallowbrook Hollow had been cancelled and the usual festivities were put on hold until Elliot had been found again.

An unhappiness spread through the Hollow. Even the pixies had stopped dancing. Elliot's disappearance had saddened everyone and everyone accepted Arlik's decision.

Chapter 6

Unbeknown to Elliot, not only had she fallen down an old hollow tree trunk but that this particular tree trunk was situated in the middle of the Weeping Woods and belonged to an old oak tree, which died when the neenarks had arrived.

The loud crash of Elliot's arrival had been heard by the neenarks and at first light, curious as to what or who had made the noise, they went to explore. Elliot was gently woken by the bright rays of sunlight, which poured through the woodpecker hole and lighted up the tree trunk that she now found herself and Nelson trapped inside. As she looked upwards towards the light, she saw several dirty faces peering back down

at her. Elliot gave a loud shriek and fell backwards in fright, banging her head on a dislodged tree root. As the dizziness flooded her head, she then fainted on top of Nelson who was still sleeping soundly, unaware of their new surroundings.

On hearing the noise coming from the old tree, Karlan, head neenark, sent Pax and Culley down through the hole and into the darkness to investigate further. The boys gently eased themselves down several dried

ivy roots, which had been twisted together to create a makeshift rope, and being very careful not to wake their mysterious stranger, they landed with care on the dusty floor beside Elliot.

Elliot stirred ever so slightly but their arrival did not fully wake her and after a few moments, when assured that she was still sleeping, Culley crept up close and sniffed at her face. Culley backed away from Elliot carefully, his dark brown eyes wide with delight, and then all of a sudden he started to leap up and down on the spot in a funny sort of dance, carefully placing his grubby little hands over his mouth as if preventing the words from breaking free. In a whisper, Culley explained to Pax that she smelt like a dewbie and if she was a dewbie, she had become their most precious prize. Both boys sniffed Elliot once more and confirming their suspicions, decided to tie Nelson's wings so their guests couldn't escape and climbed back up the rope in a hurried scramble, eagerly breaking their news to the other neenarks who were still gathered around the top.

A wave of excitement swept through the Weeping Woods at the news of this miracle and Karlan knew that Elliot was their best ever chance of lifting their curse. He also knew that they had to be wise and look after Elliot well so that she would be able to produce the finest, clearest dewdrops that they each needed to taste in order to secure their freedom. So Karlan sent Pax and Culley back down into the old tree truck with wild berries and fresh water and waited in anticipation for news of Elliot's waking and, more importantly, if there were any signs of dewdrops.

Karlan was the oldest neenark and assumed leadership. He was very bossy and disapproved of the fun and games the others played to

pass the time. He had bronzed skin, brown tangled shoulder length hair, grey eyes and a mouth, which curled downwards, making him look cross. He wore a tiny gold coin on a cord around his neck, which he had won from a leprechaun many years ago, believing that one day it would buy him his freedom.

Elliot woke first and as she opened her eyes into the semi-darkness, she realised that what she had initially thought was a dream, was in fact reality and both her and Nelson were still stuck at the bottom of a dark hole. As she looked around the dusty space, she noticed her meal served inside an upturned toadstool, with an acorn of fresh water at its side and crawled over for a closer inspection. Elliot's hunger fought with her suspicions and won. The feast looked tempting and she decided that she would worry about who had left it for her when her belly was full again.

So, she gave Nelson a sharp nudge to wake him from his sleep and the pair tucked into the berries, wondering how they were going to get out.

After a little while, and several frustrating minutes of trying to untie Nelson's wings without success, Elliot became angry and started to shout towards the opening, in the hope that one of the dirty faces would appear and she could demand their release. Elliot's cries were not in vain and Culley, who was left on guard above, heard Elliot's shouting and ran off to fetch Pax.

Culley had a gentle nature and was saddened by the dark life he was forced to live in the Weeping Woods and yearned to be reunited again with the other fairy folk at Mallowbrook Hollow. He had bright golden spiky hair, unusual deep brown eyes and a cheeky smile, which lit up his dirty little face and left the drabness of his clothes unnoticed.

Pax was slightly older, taller and more slender. He had thick copper coloured curls, pink cheeks and blue eyes. Pax carried a tiny pebble with him, which he considered to be a lucky charm. It was given to him by a dewbie when he was a young child and was one of the fondest memories of his past life as a fairy in Mallowbrook.

The boys ran towards the tree and peered down the hole; Elliot squealed again but this time managed not to faint and spent several moments studying their faces, gradually realising just who was staring back at her: Neenarks! Horror overwhelmed Elliot and she started to cry. This was far worse than she had ever imagined; not only was she in the hands of her enemy but she had found herself in a dark lonely place, far from her friends and family, who would never know she was there.

Darkness was obviously falling around the woods because the light shining through the hole became weaker. The dirty faces, as Elliot called them, had disappeared again and she was left in the darkness with Nelson, her best friend, her only friend. Elliot needed to think and she couldn't think when it was so dark. So she pulled out her silver spoon and began sprinkling dewdrops, as many as she could make. High and low, she scattered the tiny droplets, hoping that in quantity they would shine and sparkle, lighting up their new home but nothing happened. Elliot looked at Nelson puzzled and she wandered over to the tiny droplets for a closer inspection. Each and every dew drop was cloudy and grey, full to the brim with Elliot's sad thoughts. Everything seemed hopeless and Elliot started to cry again.

Chapter 7

Karlan was informed immediately by Culley and Pax that Elliot had woken but that she was in a very bad mood and Karlan knew that Elliot was unlikely to produce pure dewdrops if she was saddened. So, they waited until Elliot's sobs drifted away and tender snores took their place and Karlan sent Culley back down the ivy rope with armfuls of berries, in hope that their offering would lighten Elliot's mood.

This pattern went on for several nights; the neenarks would wait for Elliot to drift off to sleep, then Culley would quietly venture down the trunk to leave food and water, checking to see if the dewdrops had changed colour, then report his findings to a somewhat dissatisfied Karlan, waiting impatiently at the top.

Elliot was not foolish and realising this pattern, was determined to stay awake to catch the culprit but each night as she waited in the darkness, listening to the soft sounds of the woods, cuddled up to the warmth of Nelson's body, she would unwillingly fall asleep; except on this particular night.

Culley lowered himself down the rope as usual, placed the upturned toadstool full of juicy berries onto the dusty floor as usual and checked the dewdrops for any change but as usual, they remained cloudy. Then, just as he was about to clamber back up the rope again, Elliot, who had pretended to be asleep, tugged at his shabby tunic pulling Culley to the floor in front of her feet. Culley nervously smiled as he slowly looked up at Elliot who was standing over him, with her hands

on her hips and her face searching his for an explanation. Culley's smile warmed Elliot a little and she relaxed, allowing him to stand up again. As he did, Culley placed one finger up to his lips to silence Elliot and in a soft whisper asked her not to be afraid of him. He promised that he would return the next day and that she should not be scared or frightened. Then, just before he climbed back up the rope, which Pax was now wiggling furiously from the top to hurry him along, Culley patted Nelson on the top of his head and gave Elliot another broad smile.

Culley kept his promise and each night returned with wild berries and fresh water trying his hardest to make Elliot happy, not just because he knew the magic would only work if her dewdrops were clear but because he hated that she remained so sad. Sometimes he even managed to sneak away on his own so that he could

spend longer with her. Elliot liked Culley and even though their time together was limited, a friendship developed and after a while, Elliot learnt that neenarks weren't that bad after all. In fact, Culley and his friends were desperate to prove that they could be honest and kind, they just needed forgiveness and someone to trust that they had changed. Karlan, however, was different. His only interest was to break the curse by holding Elliot prisoner, believing that in time she would be forced to produce clear dewdrops and although he was angry that Culley's efforts were not making any difference, he would not give up on his only hope.

As time went on, Elliot met and made friends with the other neenarks and decided that if she ever managed to go back home again, she would beg Arlik for their freedom, believing that they had been punished for long enough.

Yelib had a roly poly tummy and a chubby face, which blushed bright red when he was in Elliot's company. Elliot noticed that his clothes were too small for him as his tummy poked out beneath his tunic and his leggings finished just below his knees, showing off his stripy socks. Elliot thought him quite a funny looking character.

Eward and Tab were brothers and were similar in appearance. Both had wavy black hair, although Tab's hair was slightly longer. Both were tall but not slender, instead they were strong and muscular, which reminded Elliot of her father.

Myer and Kiku were girls, which had shocked Elliot because she thought neenarks were all boys. Elliot could imagine how both Myer and Kiku had looked as fairies because they were light and dainty with cute little faces. Myer's hair was golden and curled on top of her head

and Kiku's hair was short, dark and spiky, which Elliot thought made her look more like a pixie.

Filmore was the youngest neenark and rarely spoke. He was exceptionally shy and he never stayed with Elliot long enough for her to get to know him. He had a long pointed nose, large ears and wispy hair and was often bullied by Karlan. Elliot learnt from Culley that Filmore spent most of his time alone in the forest, carving animals out of wood and imagining them to be his friends.

Culley and his friends all grew to love Elliot and took it in turns to spend time with her. They even asked Karlan to release her, believing that she could be trusted to stay with them until such a time that she became happy enough to produce fresh dewdrops again. But their pleas were ignored; Karlan could not risk their only hope to disappear from under their pointed noses and so

Elliot and Nelson remained trapped below ground, at the bottom of an old tree trunk for what seemed like forever.

Chapter 8

It was cold now and snowflakes were falling heavily across the wood. Elliot's only warmth was from Nelson but even he was shivering. The days were short and the nights long and Elliot lived for the brief lull to the blackness when the watery winter sun shone through the hole and down into their prison cell.

The days trapped inside the Weeping Woods all merged into one long day and Elliot had become unaware of time. Briefly, because any longer than a few moments saddened her heart, she allowed herself a moment to remember her family and friends at Mallowbrook, then realised that she had probably missed the Christmas celebrations.

The coldness outside told her that they were deep into winter and that it was now probably January or even February. Saddened by her thoughts, she carefully went over to the little pile of berries, which Yelib had left for her earlier and emptied them into one of her tiny hands, then ripped a corner of fabric from her yellow dress, placed the berries inside and gently folded the cloth to make a parcel. Elliot gave Nelson a tender kiss on his nose and wished him a very merry Christmas, placing the little gift beside him. As she snuggled up once more under his wings, she realised Nelson was crying; beautiful sparkling tears were falling down his face and splashing onto Elliot's head. Quickly, she crawled in the darkness towards the acorn shell, grabbed it and gently held it up to one of Nelson's eyes to collect the precious droplets because she knew that not only were dragonfly tears the rarest of all but that one could see their future inside them.

Elliot eagerly waited for the morning light and as the first of the sun's rays broke through the woodpecker hole, lighting up the space around her, she sat with crossed legs, the acorn shell nestled into her lap and began to sing:

Dragonfly tear, dragonfly tear,
open your secrets and bring them near.
Please show me my future,
there's no need to fear.
Dragonfly tear, dragonfly tear.

As Elliot opened her eyes and looked deep into the silvery water, she could see her brave father on his caterfiddle and Arlik and his soldiers charging through the woods on what appeared to be dragonflies. She could just make out that they were searching the Weeping Woods and calling out her name.

Excitedly, Elliot wondered if she should allow herself to believe what she was seeing unfold before her in the tears, their rescue, and with a secret smile decided to trust that they would soon be going home.

What Elliot didn't realise was that when a dragonfly cried it stirred a special kind of magic within other dragonflies and Nelson's crying had alerted Fluster, Bouncer and all of the other dragonflies in Mallowbrook. Their strange unsettled behaviour suggested they were troubled by something important, which made Ludo suspicious. Desperate to try anything to find his daughter, he called upon all of the other soldiers including Arlik, who demanded to go and handed them each a dragonfly. Somewhat confused they climbed aboard and in an excited flash the pets sped off towards the Weeping Woods. Ludo lead the way on his caterfiddle, which he chose for its

speed and strength, just in case there was trouble ahead. Arlik was given Fluster and was asked by Ludo to stay close behind him for protection.

Faster and faster they flew, the cold winter air freezing the path of their travels and as they came upon the edge of Mallowbrook Hollow, an uncertainty slowed their pace. Stretched out ahead lay the unwelcoming darkness of the Weeping Woods and the pets were all reluctant

to go on. All except Fluster, whose speed never slowed and who ignored the uncertainty he felt inside because he knew that they had to keep going: Elliot and Nelson were trapped in the creepy woods somewhere and they had to find them. Suddenly Fluster became the bravest of all dragonflies and charged across the border. Arlik wrapped his arms tightly around Fluster's neck and buried his head into the warmth of his body to block out the cold wind which was chilling his pointed ears.

Surprised by Fluster's bravery, the other pets followed closely behind, trusting their leader's decision, whilst Ludo slowed the pace to a graceful glide, searching every inch of the woods for a sign that Elliot might be there.

The Weeping Woods was every bit as unloved as Ludo thought it might be; most of the plants had died long ago and only the very hardiest

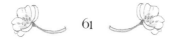

survived. There was no merriment or laughter and the freshly fallen snow created a bleakness around them, one which Ludo struggled to believe his precious daughter was trapped inside.

Chapter 9

Elliot and Culley sat side by side on the dusty floor sharing berries with Nelson, who was curled up asleep at their feet, all unaware of the wood's new visitors. She had decided not to tell Culley of Nelson's tears and what she had seen within them, after all, it was probably just hope that had brought her the visions of their rescue and she didn't want to alarm Culley unnecessarily and she certainly didn't want Karlan finding out.

Suddenly, and without warning, Nelson jumped up as though something loud had woken him, causing the friends to giggle. Elliot stoked his slender back to sooth him but Nelson didn't calm. In fact, he

began making a clicking noise, which Elliot had not heard before. Nelson's behaviour was unusual and Elliot felt excitement overflow her thoughts and wondered if this could be their rescue, could this be everything she had wished for over the past few months?

Nelson's clicking got louder and louder, which made Culley suspicious and as he turned to Elliot, he noticed happiness in Elliot's eyes for the first time, happiness which had been missing before and he knew something was about to change.

Culley clambered up the rope and out of the woodpecker hole, despite Elliot's efforts to pull him back again and ran to get the other neenarks. Elliot, knowing that this could be her only chance of freedom, started calling upwards towards the hole, now hoping that the visions shown to her in Nelson's tears were about to become true.

Alerted by Elliot's cries and Nelson's clicking, in one swoop, Fluster circled the old tree trunk which was holding Elliot and Nelson prisoners and without any hesitation, Ludo and his caterfiddle disappeared down the hole, landing on top of Nelson with a loud thump. Elliot ran to her father who swept her off her feet and held her tightly inside one of his big hugs. Elliot knew instantly that she was safe and the months of worry that had lived with Ludo vanished in an instant. Ludo's strength untied Nelson's wings and in an unsteady wobble Nelson flew upwards and out of the hole, followed closely by Ludo and Elliot, all joining brave Fluster outside.

Ludo lowered Elliot to the snow covered ground and watched her with fatherly pride as she spent a few moments smelling the fresh air and enjoying her freedom. Elliot's rescuers cheered and clapped as she danced and swirled around with happiness, which filled her and as she pulled out her tiny silver spoon, clear fresh dewdrops cascaded around them, glistening sweetly as they landed on the dried plants, which had dared to poke through the icy snow.

Their celebrations were sharply interrupted by Karlan, who was also clapping but with evil amusement and he marched right up to Arlik and stood before him. The other neenarks watched in anticipation from behind the bushes and trees, truly amazed at the rare sight of fresh dewdrops so temptingly close around them.

Karlan was in no mood to be friendly with his enemy and immediately demanded that their curse was lifted. Arlik explained that he would lift their curse on the understanding that they were all ready to be kind and honest. Then, with a wave of his hands he produced nine fresh green oak leaves, which fell to the floor in

front of them. Arlik beckoned the neenarks one by one to take an oak leaf and fill it with the dewdrops Elliot had just made. If it were true that they had a pure, kind heart, then as the dew touched their lips they would be returned to the fairy they once were. If, however, they were still selfish and unkind, nothing would happen and they would remain cursed.

The neenarks formed a line and in turn each took an oak leaf and filled it with dewdrops. Elliot watched as Culley went first. Nervously he poured the sweet liquid into his tiny mouth and then in a flash of the brightest light he became a fairy again, full of colour, sparkle and happiness.

Pax, Yelib, Eward, Tab, Myer, Kiku and Filmore all patiently waited for their turn and one by one proved to Arlik that they were worthy to become fairies again. Elliot clapped with excitement.

Karlan was last and he grabbed

the remaining leaf and scooped as many dewdrops as he could, quickly pouring the dew into his mouth. They waited but nothing happened. So he scooped up the remaining droplets but just as he was about to put the leaf up to his lips it disappeared. Culley and the others gasped.

Arlik explained that the leaf had disappeared because Karlan had not changed. He had not learnt to be kind and honest and therefore the curse could not be lifted. Arlik held his arms into the air and muttered a spell.

Selfish fairy I cast this spell
and banish you to the Old Wishing
Well

With a flash, Karlan disappeared. Arlik had banished him to the Old Wishing Well, which sat in the furthest corner of the Weeping Woods, in a faraway place, where no one visited

and where no magic existed. Karlan would remain alone, unloved and never allowed to leave as punishment for how he treated Elliot.

Elliot felt sad for Karlan as she had hoped that he too had learnt to be kind but knew that Arlik was a wise elf and if he thought Karlan was still unkind, then she had to accept his decision.

It was time to leave and head back home. Elliot was tired now and decided to ride with her father, allowing Culley and Pax to fly Nelson home. The other neenarks rode with the other soldiers and as they began to fly, Arlik cast another spell returning the Weeping Woods back into Fernfuddle Forest again. Once Arlik's magic dust had settled over the plants and trees, fresh green shoots started to appear, birds sang and tiny animals ventured out of their underground homes and into the sunshine.

Fernfuddle Forest was again a

beautiful, welcoming place, full of the things that made Elliot happy and as she took one last glimpse at Fernfuddle her eyes gave up the fight to stay open and she drifted into a peaceful sleep, leaving Arlik and Fluster to lead everyone back home to safety.

Chapter 10

Elliot had no memory of their journey home that day, unaware that her sleep was so deep that Ludo had managed to gently carry her into their home without waking her. Arlik cast a gentle sleeping spell over Elliot to help her rest peacefully and regain both energy and spirit.

Elliot was also unaware that whilst she was trapped in the Weeping Woods, not only had she missed Christmas but she had missed her birthday too and whilst she slept, the fairy folk of Mallowbrook Hollow decided that Elliot's safe return, their postponed Christmas and her missed birthday should all be celebrated with one big party and as winter quickly turned into spring everyone became busy with the

party preparations. Needless to say, news of a party excited the pixies.

Dixie and Boo took it in turns to sit with Elliot at her bedside, reading poems from their favourite book, Dawn combed her long auburn hair each morning and tied new yellow ribbons at the ends of her pigtails and Culley came every day with armfuls of fresh berries, just as he used to when she was in the woods.

Lillianna was busy organising the party preparations. She instructed the fairies to drape bright yellow garlands and ribbons around Mallowbrook Hollow, the leprechauns to take over from the gnomes to collect shiny sweet wrappers for the presents and the elves to pick berries and nuts for the feast. This left the gnomes busy with a pile of broken twigs, leaves and tree bark building something extra special for the celebration. As usual, the pixies danced but this time no one seemed to mind.

Everything was carefully planned and Arlik announced that this celebration was for Elliot, to celebrate her love of Christmas, her affection for the spring and the summer and yellow, her favourite colour but most of all, to celebrate that she had been found safe and sound.

Chapter 11

After many weeks of hard work and organising the celebrations were ready to begin and on the last Monday of May the sun shone, the birds sang, spring was breaking into summer and Arlik woke Elliot from her slumber.

Elliot yawned a huge yawn and rubbed her tired eyes as she slowly opened them noticing very quickly that she was surrounded by everyone she loved most-her family and friends.

In an excited flurry of cheers and happy tears, Dixie and Boo hugged Elliot eager to know about her adventures and Dawn and Ludo each gave her a tender kiss on her pink little cheeks. Echo and Bear jumped happily up and down on Elliot's bed and Culley swept her a bow as he handed her an acorn shell full to the brim with berries whilst smiling one of his widest smiles.

Elliot noticed Arlik standing towards the back of the crowd, which had gathered around her and as she looked towards him, he gave her a little wink as if to tell her everything was going to be ok. Elliot also noticed that she was dressed in her finest yellow clothes and looked to Dawn for an explanation. Dawn, however, just smiled sweetly and tapped her finger to the side of her nose as if to say it was a secret that couldn't be shared just yet.

Ludo ushered everyone out of his home, so that they could get ready for Elliot's surprise and he took Elliot by the hand and pulled her close to him for a huge hug because Ludo above everyone else was pleased that this day had finally come.

Nelson was excitedly waiting outside

for Elliot and pranced about in a funny sort of dance when he saw her. She ran over and gave him a big hug and tickled his belly, which he particularly liked. She whispered a special thank you for looking after her and especially for his tears, just when they needed them most of all and which gave her the hope she needed.

Nelson dropped to his knees allowing Elliot to climb onto his back and in an upwards spin, which made Elliot giggle, they flew towards the sundial. On their journey, she noticed the bright yellow garlands draped from the trees and plants and wondered what they were for. She also heard the music playing from underneath the sundial as they landed close by.

The pair were met by Lillianna, who gently covered Elliot's eyes with her soft hands then carefully guided her towards the sundial and the eerie

silence, which had now fallen across the Hollow. Elliot was curiously excited and tried unsuccessfully to open her eyes beneath Lillianna's fingers to take a peek. Then all of a sudden, making Elliot jump, everyone shouted "surprise!"

Elliot stood frozen, unable to speak and slowly looked around at the yellow bows and garlands which hung neatly around the sundial, she noticed the feast of berries and nuts waiting to be eaten and what appeared to be a huge pyramid proudly sitting in the middle of the floor, covered from top to bottom in a patchwork of shiny sweet wrappers. Arlik approached her, took her tiny hands in his and wished her a happy Ellimas; Elliot's Christmas.

As everyone cheered and clapped, the elves started to play their music, which made the pixies dance and all of the dewbies flew up and over the sundial, sprinkling thousands of

dewdrops, which exploded like watery fireworks. Finally and just before the procession began, Arlik stood at the pyramid and raising his hands high in the air, he announced the opening of the Ellimas celebrations and with a loud flash, the pyramid burst open and hundreds of beautifully wrapped gifts cascaded out of the top, showering everyone with presents.

Elliot was the happiest she had ever been. A celebration had been made especially for her honouring all the things she loved the best and she was truly happy.

The party went on into the night and everyone had fun, even Ludo was seen clapping in time to the music, which made Dawn smile. As Elliot sat next to Culley on an old tree stump underneath the stars, with Nelson curled at their feet, she looked up into the sky and thanked whoever made it possible for her to have such a wonderful life.

So now you know the story of Ellimas, Elliot's Christmas, a celebration of spring turning to summer and to honour a special little dewbie called Elliot.

So make a note to remember the last Monday of every May because if you are extremely lucky, you may just witness Ellimas celebrations taking place at the bottom of your own garden.